CRAZY WORLD PRODUCTIONS, INC.

AuthorHouse™
1663 Liberty Drive
Bloomington, IN 47403
www.authorhouse.com
Phone: 1 (800) 839-8640

This book is a work of fiction. People, places, events, and situations are the product of the author's imagination. Any resemblance to actual persons, living or dead, or historical events, is purely coincidental.

Published by AuthorHouse 03/21/2017

ISBN: 978-1-4259-0300-8 (sc)

Print information available on the last page.

This book is printed on acid-free paper.

authorHOUSE

THE CRAZY WORLD OF MEDICINE

THE MADNESS BEGINS

JAY VINCENT

Other books by the author

Entering the Privacy Zone: A Robert Boston Spy Novel

Soon to be Published:

The Crazy World of Medicine: The Madness Continues
The Crazy World of Lawyers: The Court Goes Wild
Adventures of the Park Street Hounds: The Tomcat Uprising
The Shadow Hawk Project: A Robert Boston Spy Novel
Stalker and the Prey

FOR MATT

Thank you for saving me from the bustle

And then from lions in Rome

This book is for you

TABLE OF CONTENTS

Madness In The Birthing Center 1
Priest On The Prowl 2
Looting Santa's Bounty 3
A Visit From The Taliban 4
Chasing Hospital Food 5
Militia Working The Gift Cart 6
I.V. Therapy Gone Mad 7
A Smoking Experience 8
A Napolean Complexity 9
The UFO Clinic 10
Losing Your Head 11
Blind Man Down 12
The Drug Arrival 13
Get On The Hot Seat – Now! 14
ER For Nudists 15
If Smoking Was Permitted In The OR 16
Toxic Spill? 17
Surgeon General Sets The Record Straight 18
Eye Doctor From Hell 19
At Louie's Lab – Where It All Began 20
Heart Shocker On The Loose 21
Spin Cycle 22
Reflex Mania 23
Show And Tell Gone Mad 24
No More Boring Waiting Rooms 25
Rotund Santa 26
Plastic Surgery Nightmare 27
Suddenly You're A Sandwich 28

ER Waiting Area For Lawyers 29
The Wacked Out Old Curiosity Shop 30
Stethoscope Mania 31
Third Shift 32
Titanic Fever Hits The Old Folks Home 33
How Many Personalities You Got? 34
Violating Policy 35
Drive-Up Surgery 36
Hound Dog Doctor 37
Like Pulling Teech 38
Baldash And The Devil 39
A Pre-Surgical Toast 40
Inkblot Distress 41
A Warhead On 2-South 42
Jolly Green Patient 43
The Infamous Elephant Nose 44
Really Strange Doctor Rounds 45
Surgical Suite Capers 46
Hospital Tissue Bank 47
Bedpan Shortage 48
Patient Anxiety 49
Short Staffed Again 50
Really Bad Bedside Manners 51
Elopement Risk 52
Overstressed And Overworked 53
Take A Neck Reading? 54
Got The Narc' Keys? 55
An Apple A Day 56

Doctor Jack On The Loose Again...........57
Bloodsucker...........58
Just Heimlich Everyone...........59
Casino ER...........60
Hospital Corridor Bowling...........61
Zombie Slip...........62
Super Healer...........63
Horse Pills...........64
Fashion And Hospital Gowns...........65
Fun With The Defibrillator...........66
Curing Hiccups...........67
Fuzzheads On The Ward...........68
Fresh Air Freak...........69
Medical Receptionist From Hell...........70
Marketing Medicine...........71
A Robbery At The Pharmacy...........72
A Bad Practical Joke...........73
Finbacks On The Unit...........74
Paperwork First!...........75
Wrong Direction...........76
Neurosurgeons At Large...........77
Fund With Samples...........78
Finding Hoffa...........79
The Godfather And His Cronies Take Up Medicine...........80
The Hate Filled Presentation...........81
Take A Flight...........82
The Eye Test...........83
Trouble With Catheters...........84
Whoa! Census Is Down...........85
Doctor, Control Yourself...........86
Ridin' The Call Light...........87
Compassion, What's That?...........88
Hot Headed Flo Nightingale...........89
Is That The Patch You're Wearing?...........90
NASCAR Gurney...........91
Overactive Electric Bed...........92
Making Your Toes Feel Better...........93
Hot Shots...........94
Fun With Gas...........95
The Hair Doctor...........96
Animal Hospital...........97
Prank Stat Call...........98
Administrator Gone Nuts...........99
Lawyers' Ward...........100

THE CRAZY WORLD OF MEDICINE by Jay Vincent

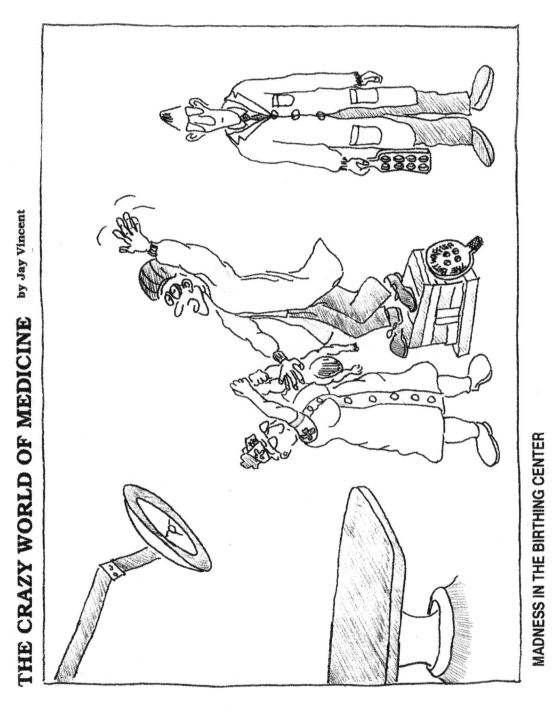

MADNESS IN THE BIRTHING CENTER

The Birthing Center's new Butt Pounding Team gets started.

THE CRAZY WORLD OF MEDICINE by Jay Vincent

PRIEST ON THE PROWL

"I thought I'd stop by to offer a word of prayer but now that I've met you, uh, maybe not."

THE CRAZY WORLD OF MEDICINE   by Jay Vincent

LOOTING SANTA'S BOUNTY

With the big guy out like a light, the ER staff took advantage and quickly made up for the disappointments of X-Mas past.

THE CRAZY WORLD OF MEDICINE   by Jay Vincent

A VISIT FROM THE TALIBAN

In a display of bad business judgment, Hospital administration fired the Shriners and replaced them with recently unemployed members of the Taliban.

THE CRAZY WORLD OF MEDICINE by Jay Vincent

CHASING HOSPITAL FOOD

"Good thing barbecued critter sells so well and everybody likes mystery ribs."

THE CRAZY WORLD OF MEDICINE   by Jay Vincent

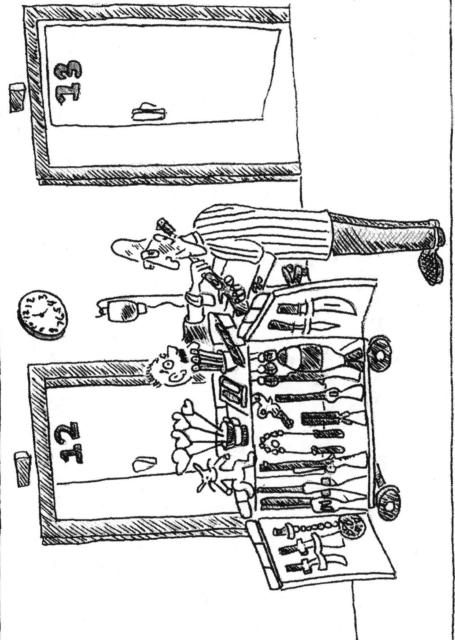

MILITIA WORKING THE GIFT CART

"All right, so you want the rifle instead of the torpedo and remember, you can fire this sucker right from your hospital bed. Godspeed, brother."

THE CRAZY WORLD OF MEDICINE   by Jay Vincent

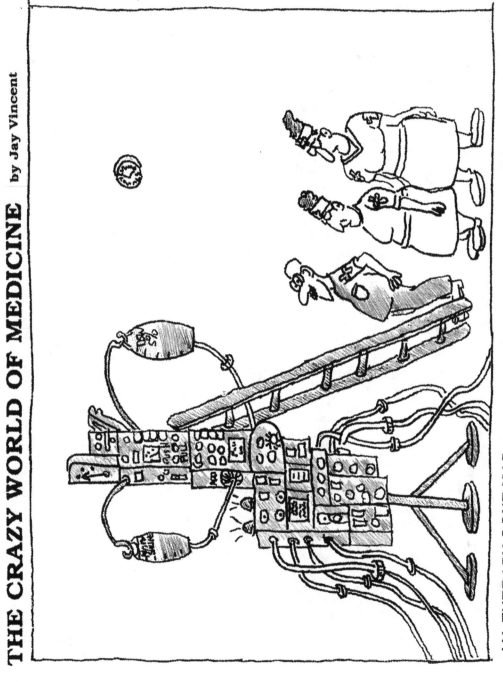

I.V. THERAPY GONE MAD

"Awe, com'n, this new IV pump doesn't look that complicated. It's all in the way you look at it!"

THE CRAZY WORLD OF MEDICINE   by Jay Vincent

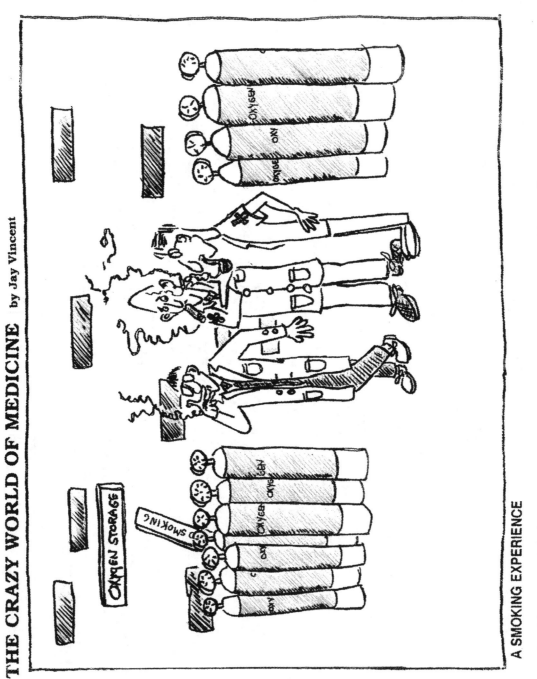

A SMOKING EXPERIENCE

"Who'd have thunk it that the Hospital Committee Against Smoking would actually designate a place for us to smoke!"

THE CRAZY WORLD OF MEDICINE by Jay Vincent

A NAPOLEON COMPLEXITY

"Heck no I don't think I'm Napoleon or anything, I only wear this uniform because my French Armies expect it from a General of my stature!"

THE CRAZY WORLD OF MEDICINE by Jay Vincent

THE UFO CLINIC

Anxious to be first for free treatment, the Zenith Z3 from Mars crashed into the clinic at 300 warp speed, spilling aliens everywhere.

THE CRAZY WORLD OF MEDICINE by Jay Vincent

LOSING YOUR HEAD

Tired of his handicap, Sleepy Hollow's most famous resident finally opted for treatment.

THE CRAZY WORLD OF MEDICINE by Jay Vincent

BLIND MAN DOWN

"Hey, I know you're blind, Mr. Blockhead, but you've gotta move a little bit faster if your butt's gonna catch this chair. Got that!"

THE CRAZY WORLD OF MEDICINE by Jay Vincent

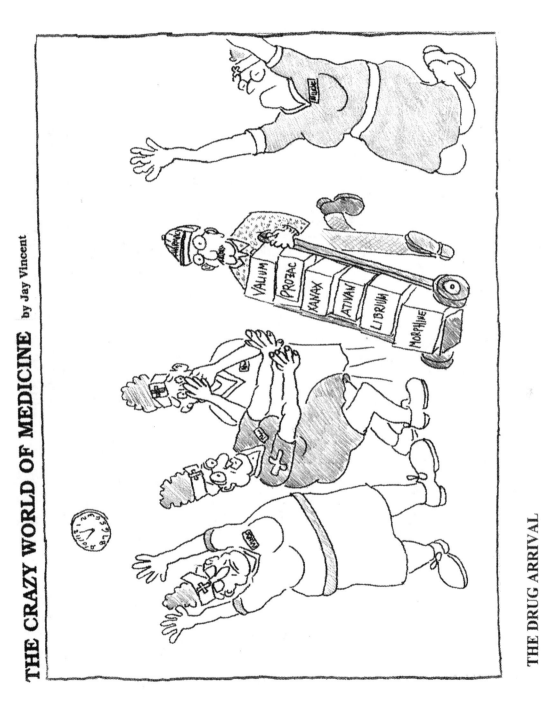

THE DRUG ARRIVAL
"Get the chant started, ladies, 'cause the happy pills are here!"

THE CRAZY WORLD OF MEDICINE by Jay Vincent

GET ON THE HOT SEAT - NOW!

"All right, listen, docs. I've got this nagging burning sensation, got it at my workplace, and I'm wonderin' if you've got a cream or lotion or maybe a nice little salve to put on it. Make that industrial strength if you know what I mean."

THE CRAZY WORLD OF MEDICINE by Jay Vincent

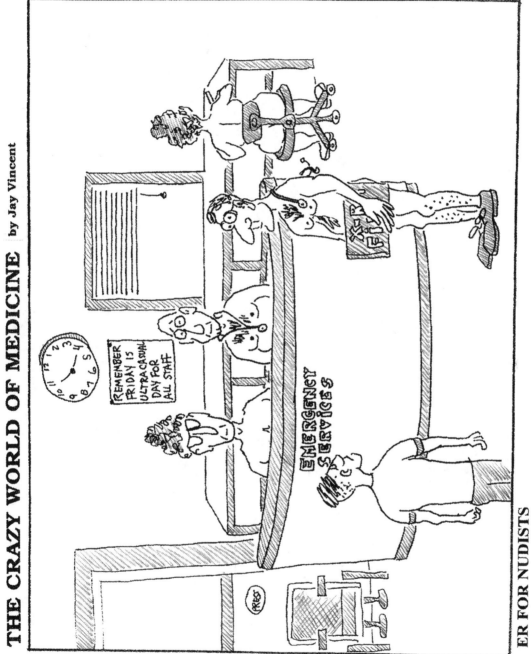

ER FOR NUDISTS
"Where do we put our name badges? Well, young man, that's a good question."

THE CRAZY WORLD OF MEDICINE By Jay Vincent

IF SMOKING WAS PERMITTED IN THE OPERATING ROOM

"Here you go, Doctor, one last puff before you open him up."

THE CRAZY WORLD OF MEDICINE · by Jay Vincent

TOXIC SPILL?

"Stand back, ma'am, this is a hospital lunch and that means this is a job for the toxic spill team."

THE CRAZY WORLD OF MEDICINE   by Jay Vincent

SURGEON GENERAL SETS THE RECORD STRAIGHT
"No, no, no! I said *surfing* can be hazardous to your health, that's *surfing*, not smoking now light my Camel and let's get back to work."

THE CRAZY WORLD OF MEDICINE by Jay Vincent

EYE DOCTOR FROM HELL

"All right, all right, now go ahead and read that second line but don't take it personal, monkey butt."

THE CRAZY WORLD OF MEDICINE by Jay Vincent

AT LOUIE'S LAB ~ WHERE IT ALL BEGAN
Suddenly, Crazy Louie Pasteur got some bad milk and became the butt of every lab joke thereafter.

THE CRAZY WORLD OF MEDICINE by Jay Vincent

HEART SHOCKER ON THE LOOSE

"Merry Christmas! Looks like Mister Jack-In-The-Box got your old ticker trottin' along there, huh?"

THE CRAZY WORLD OF MEDICINE   by Jay Vincent

SPIN CYCLE
If I can do what I want to with my break time, I want another ride in the spin cycle so shut the door."

THE CRAZY WORLD OF MEDICINE by Jay Vincent

REFLEX MANIA

"Hurt your knee, what? It's just a simple reflex test so brace up and stop your snivelling."

THE CRAZY WORLD OF MEDICINE · by Jay Vincent

SHOW AND TELL GONE MAD

To make matters worse, the Chief of Staff took advantage of show and tell day at the hospital to bring in his pet elephant which wreaked havoc on the emergency room.

THE CRAZY WORLD OF MEDICINE by Jay Vincent

NO MORE BORING WAITING ROOMS
"What, you're bored waiting for the doctor? Well snap outa it 'cause we're here to keep you busy so you don't get bored!"

THE CRAZY WORLD OF MEDICINE by Jay Vincent

ROTUND SANTA
"All right, Santa, hand over those cookies and that milk! You want to get stuck in another chimney or what?"

THE CRAZY WORLD OF MEDICINE   by Jay Vincent

PLASTIC SURGERY NIGHTMARE

"Jeez, Bob, your face lift ad did great but looking at this line-up maybe I should ask if your plastic surgery skills are, uh, up to snuff."

THE CRAZY WORLD OF MEDICINE by Jay Vincent

SUDDENLY YOU'RE A SANDWICH
"Don't look now, Ted, but your sandwich board is having you for lunch."
Everybody, even sandwich boards, love a snack now and then.

THE CRAZY WORLD OF MEDICINE by Jay Vincent

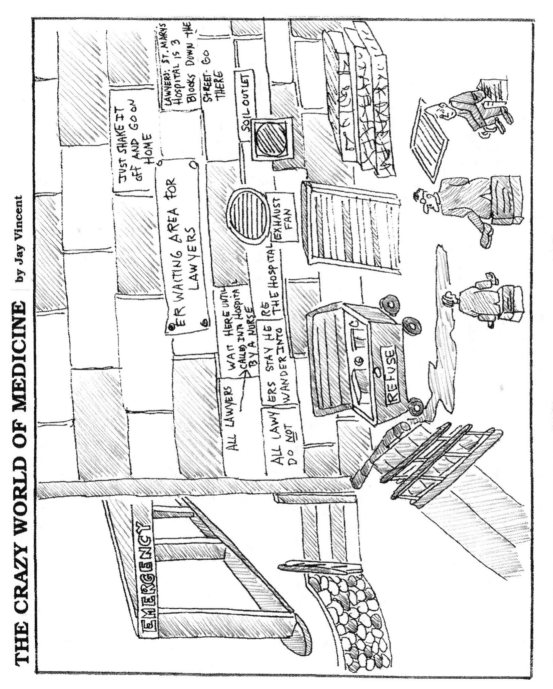

ER WAITING AREA FOR LAWYERS

THE CRAZY WORLD OF MEDICINE by Jay Vincent

THE WACKED OUT OLD CURIOSITY SHOP

A strange and curious twist on hospital gifts - gifts definitely not for the faint hearted or queasy.

THE CRAZY WORLD OF MEDICINE by Jay Vincent

STETHOSCOPE MANIA

"But Doc, maybe you can hear five hearts at once but how will you tell which one you're hearing?"

THE CRAZY WORLD OF MEDICINE by Jay Vincent

THIRD SHIFT
Sometime after midnight, third shift gets busy.

THE CRAZY WORLD OF MEDICINE by Jay Vincent

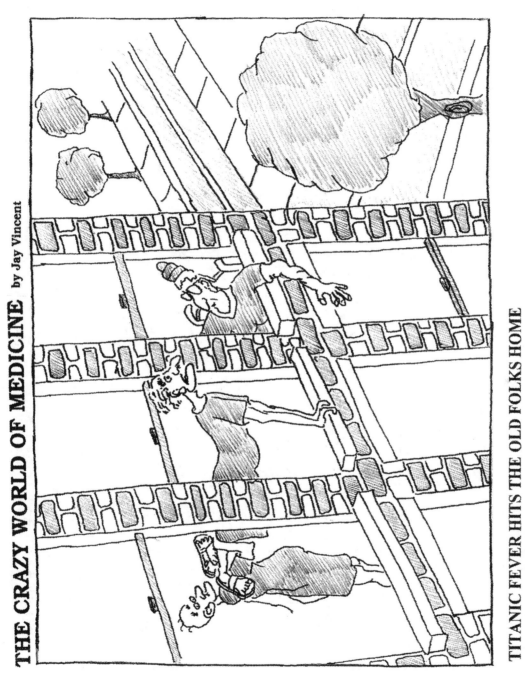

TITANIC FEVER HITS THE OLD FOLKS HOME

"Get back in that window, you fool, you're no more the King of the World than I'm the Queen of the Ball!"

THE CRAZY WORLD OF MEDICINE by Jay Vincent

HOW MANY PERSONALITIES YOU GOT?

"Okay, so let's see, you've got dual personalities so I'll have to charge you double because, hey, I'm counseling two people, you know!"

THE CRAZY WORLD OF MEDICINE   by Jay Vincent

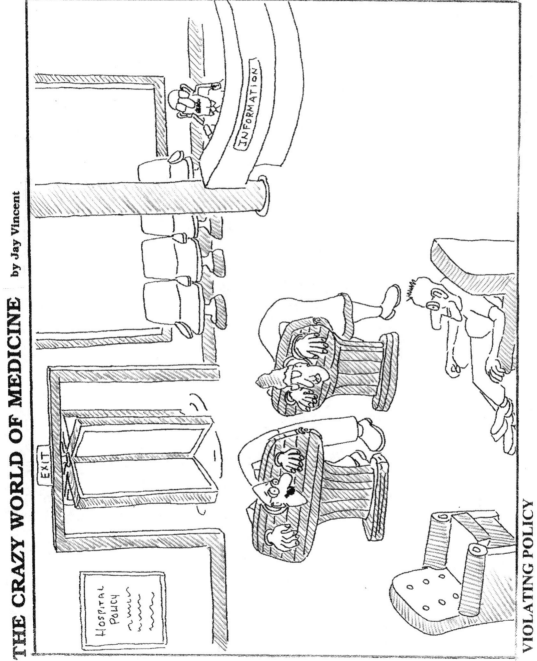

VIOLATING POLICY

"Hey, this new nurse manager is really tough on tardiness but at least it gets us off the floor."

THE CRAZY WORLD OF MEDICINE by Jay Vincent

DRIVE-UP SURGERY

Keeping overhead down, the surgical team had a bright idea involving a flashing sign and a lot next to the highway where they could get down to business.

THE CRAZY WORLD OF MEDICINE by Jay Vincent

HOUND DOG DOCTOR
"Well, Nurse Prettypants, I know I'm a charmer but I'm not sure what you mean when you say that my true character is shining through."

THE CRAZY WORLD OF MEDICINE | by Jay Vincent

LIKE PULLING TEETH
Sick of Hank's stubborn molar, Dentist Tom decided to call in the jackhammers.

THE CRAZY WORLD OF MEDICINE   by Jay Vincent

BALDASH AND THE DEVIL
After meeting the Chief of Staff, Baldash, the new student doctor somehow knew there would be trouble.

THE CRAZY WORLD OF MEDICINE by Jay Vincent

A PRE-SURGICAL TOAST
Suddenly, the surgical team realized they were prepping their 100th patient so they broke out the bubbly.

THE CRAZY WORLD OF MEDICINE — by Jay Vincent

INKBLOT DISTRESS
"But Doctor Knothead, I get the strange feeling that Mr. Rorschach doesn't like me very much."

THE CRAZY WORLD OF MEDICINE   by Jay Vincent

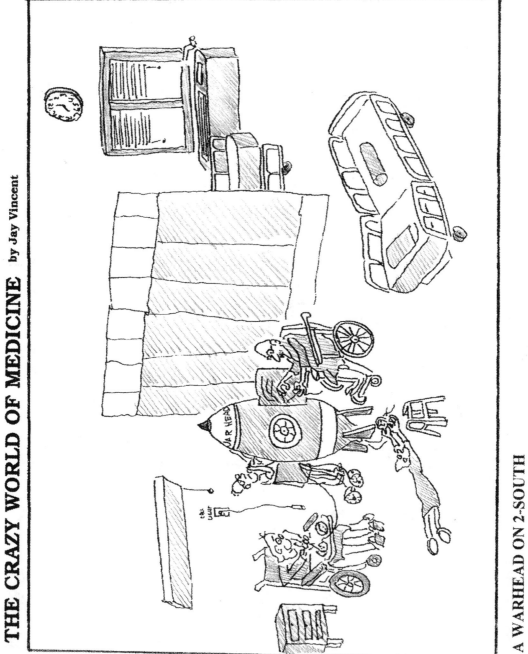

A WARHEAD ON 2-SOUTH
The men of Resident Council prepare to display their displeasure over the bad nursing home food and the 4 a.m. showers.

THE CRAZY WORLD OF MEDICINE by Jay Vincent

JOLLY GREEN PATIENT
"Awe, now look there, Pete, you forgot the handcart so we could empty this guy's urinal."

THE CRAZY WORLD OF MEDICINE by Jay Vincent

THE INFAMOUS ELEPHANT NOSE
Since Dr. Hoofensnout started wearing the infamous elephant nose, *nobody* **wanted to be "next".**

THE CRAZY WORLD OF MEDICINE
by Jay Vincent

REALLY STRANGE DOCTOR ROUNDS
"Listen, you're gonna get better and you're gonna do it now or I'm not doctoring your sorry butt anymore!"

THE CRAZY WORLD OF MEDICINE | by Jay Vincent

SURGICAL SUITE CAPERS
Rob, the new surgery intern, thought he'd earn points and get a laugh by crimping the back of Doctor Bob's knee while he was making his first cut.

THE CRAZY WORLD OF MEDICINE by Jay Vincent

HOSPITAL TISSUE BANK

THE CRAZY WORLD OF MEDICINE   by Jay Vincent

BEDPAN SHORTAGE

The strange bedpan shortage was suddenly solved when the nurses stumbled upon Houskeeper Crotchett's hidden bedpan stash.

THE CRAZY WORLD OF MEDICINE

by Jay Vincent

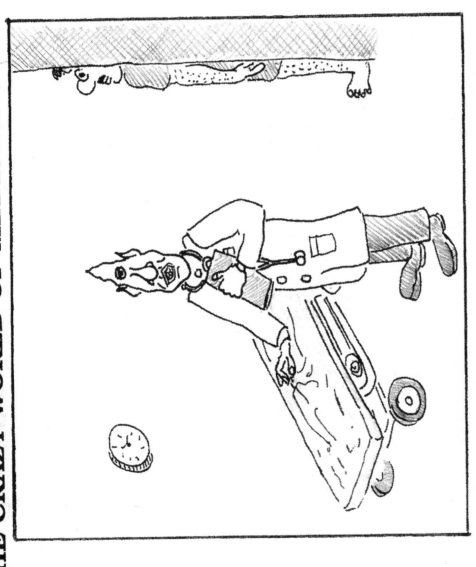

PATIENT ANXIETY

"Nurse, where's my patient? I can't understand why they all disappear."
Sadly, Doctor Cyclops loses yet another timid patient.

THE CRAZY WORLD OF MEDICINE by Jay Vincent

SHORT STAFFED AGAIN

"Look, Mable, if you can flush a few catheters and I can hold onto my walker long enough, Ralphie and I can pass pills."

THE CRAZY WORLD OF MEDICINE by Jay Vincent

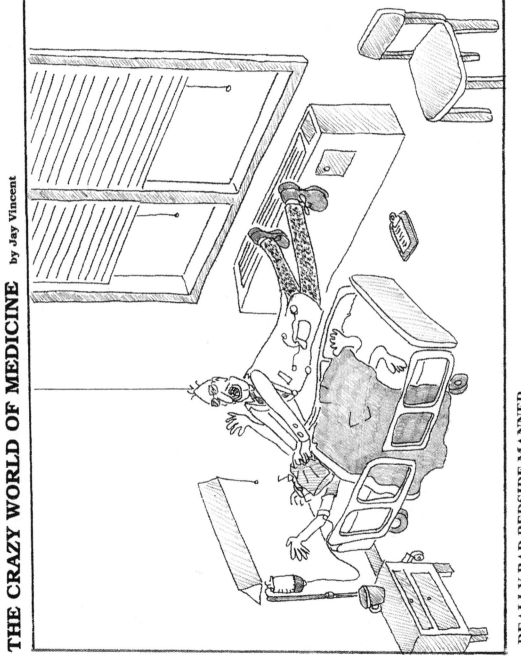

REALLY BAD BEDSIDE MANNER
Tired of Ms. Barker's bellyaching, Doctor Grief went nuts and applied the famed smothering treatment.

THE CRAZY WORLD OF MEDICINE by Jay Vincent

ELOPEMENT RISK

THE CRAZY WORLD OF MEDICINE by Jay Vincent

OVERSTRESSED AND OVERWORKED
"Alright, now hear this. You will bring all psych drugs to the nurses' station and then leave, leave, leave..."

THE CRAZY WORLD OF MEDICINE | by Jay Vincent

TAKE A NECK READING?

"No, don't worry about holding your breath, the cuff will do that for you."

THE CRAZY WORLD OF MEDICINE by Jay Vincent

GOT THE NARC KEYS?

"Uh, yes, I thought I could safeguard these narcotics better right here in the trunk of my car, officer, but thanks for your concern."

THE CRAZY WORLD OF MEDICINE by Jay Vincent

AN APPLE A DAY

"If an apple a day keeps the doctor away, dropping a 500 lb apple on his car should keep him away for at least a year, don't you think so, Al?"

THE CRAZY WORLD OF MEDICINE
by Jay Vincent

DOCTOR JACK ON THE LOOSE AGAIN
With suicides on the wane, Doctor Jack takes to the sidewalks for new prospects.

THE CRAZY WORLD OF MEDICINE   by Jay Vincent

BLOODSUCKER
"Don't look now but I think there's something odd about that new lab tech but I can't quite put my finger on it."

THE CRAZY WORLD OF MEDICINE by Jay Vincent

JUST HEIMLICH EVERYONE

Heimlich leaves after successfully maneuvering everyone in sight. Back in those days it was a privilege to be maneuvered by the great man himself and people faked choking all the time whenever he came around.

THE CRAZY WORLD OF MEDICINE by Jay Vincent

CASINO ER
"Trauma nothing, we'll get to them later. For now, there's big money at stake so hit me again, Mort!"

THE CRAZY WORLD OF MEDICINE   by Jay Vincent

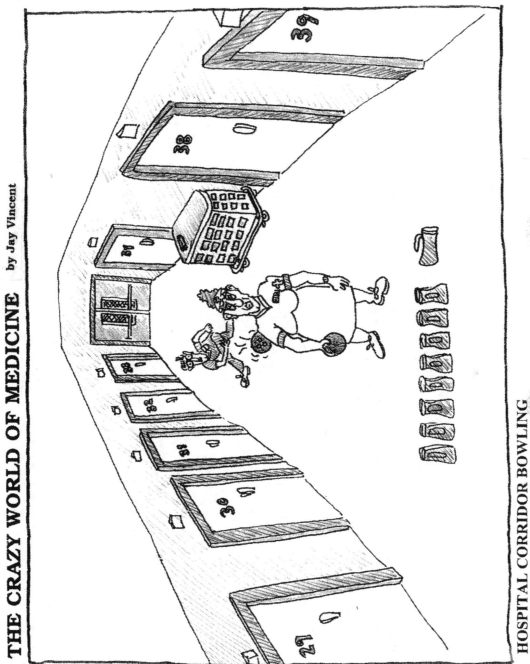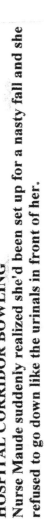

HOSPITAL CORRIDOR BOWLING
Nurse Maude suddenly realized she'd been set up for a nasty fall and she refused to go down like the urinals in front of her.

THE CRAZY WORLD OF MEDICINE   by Jay Vincent

ZOMBIE SLIP

Good old Oscar the morgue attendant knew he should have refused to see *The Sixth Sense* but he was sure his new Zombie Slip would save him from any ghouls.

THE CRAZY WORLD OF MEDICINE by Jay Vincent

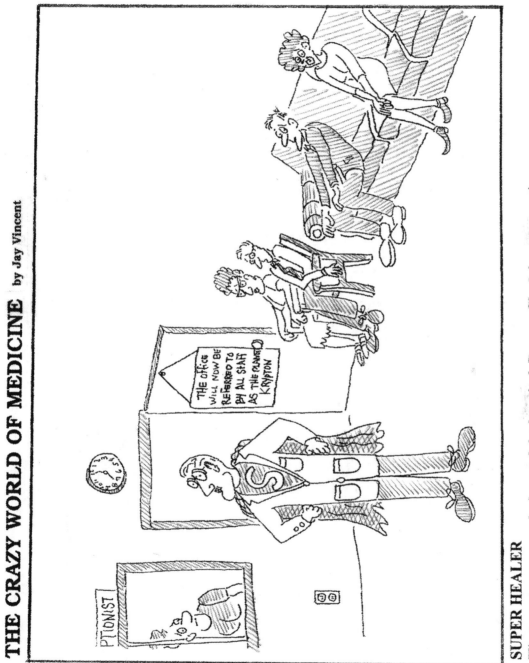

SUPER HEALER

His recent successes the buzz of the hospital, Doctor Clark began sporting an "S" on his chest, a cape, and expressing an inordinate fear in Kryptonite.

THE CRAZY WORLD OF MEDICINE | by Jay Vincent

HORSE PILLS
"I've been taking these big horse pills so long, I think I'm develping an immunity to them. Can you help me?"

THE CRAZY WORLD OF MEDICINE by Jay Vincent

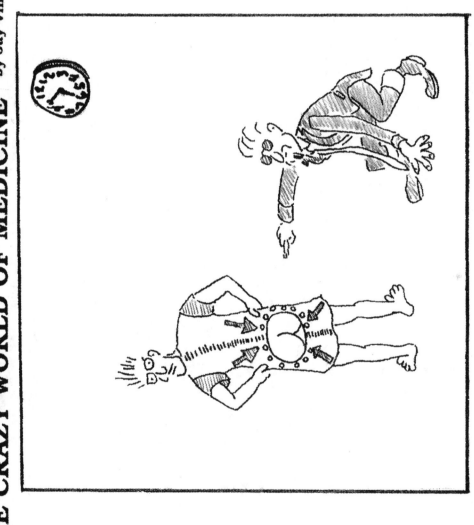

FASHION AND HOSPITAL GOWNS
Seymour Butts, fashion designer for No Privacy At All Hospital Gowns, Inc., develops yet another spectacular fashion.

THE CRAZY WORLD OF MEDICINE | by Jay Vincent

FUN WITH THE DEFIBRILLATOR
Overworked and overwrought, crazy Doctor Zano decided to treat his colleagues to a shocking experience.

THE CRAZY WORLD OF MEDICINE by Jay Vincent

CURING HICCUPS

Fed up with Johnny's incurable hiccups, the infamous Hiccup Curing Team was called out of the basement on yet another job.

THE CRAZY WORLD OF MEDICINE   by Jay Vincent

FUZZHEADS ON THE WARD

Bored by their pursuit of medicine, the student doctors tried their hand at hairstyling.

THE CRAZY WORLD OF MEDICINE by Jay Vincent

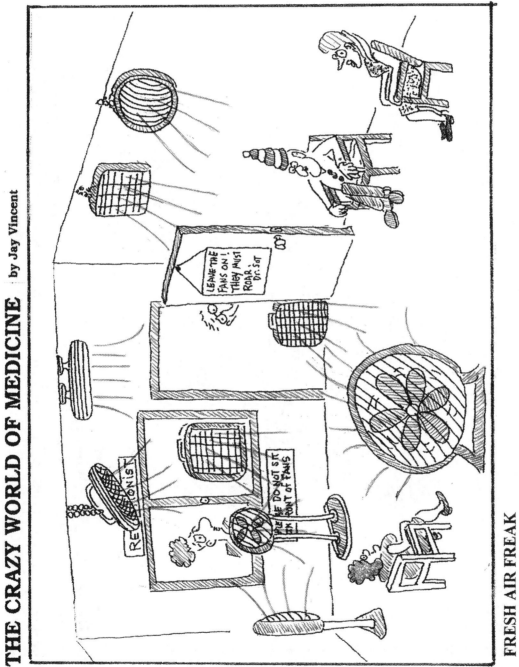

FRESH AIR FREAK

"Doctor Pimpleknees threatened to take the fronts off all the fans if we complained. That would really give us something to worry about, he said."

THE CRAZY WORLD OF MEDICINE | by Jay Vincent

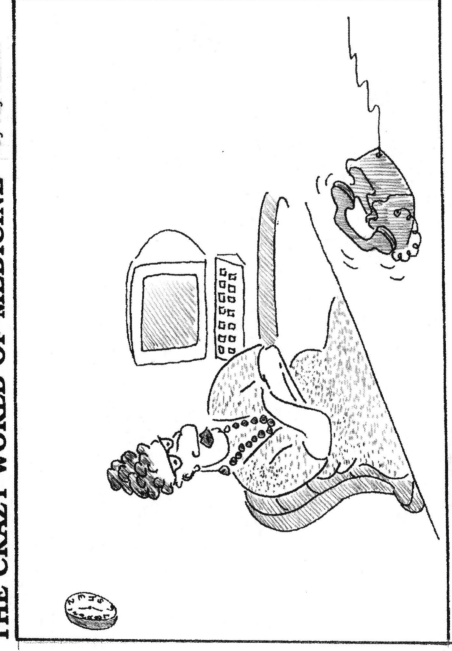

MEDICAL RECEPTIONIST FROM HELL
Caught in a daze and uncertain about the strange ringing noise coming from the plastic box in front of her, the new medical receptionist played it cool and elected to do nothing.

THE CRAZY WORLD OF MEDICINE by Jay Vincent

MARKETING MEDICINE
Doctor Kutanslice treated his new patients to a surprise and introduced them to his pet crocs which he always kept around the office.

THE CRAZY WORLD OF MEDICINE by Jay Vincent

A ROBBERY AT THE PHARMACY

"These pills you sold me, since they taste like chocolate and have a colorful candy coating, shouldn't they have cost me the M&M price?"

THE CRAZY WORLD OF MEDICINE by Jay Vincent

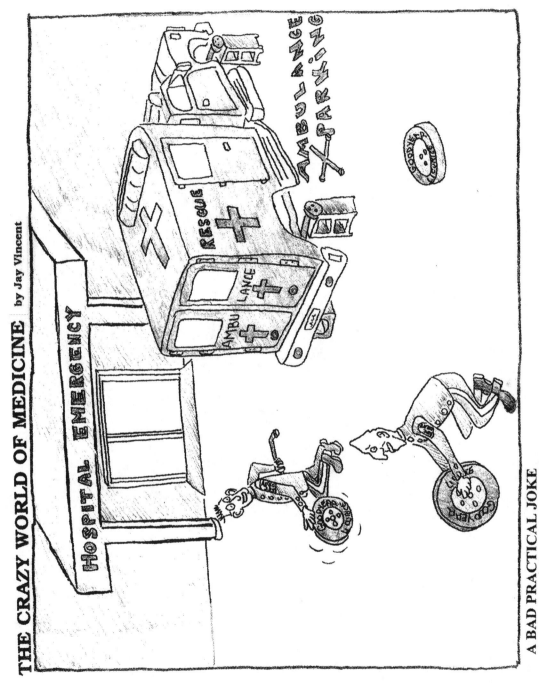

A BAD PRACTICAL JOKE

"Hah, hah, wait 'till they get a load of this. We'll get 'em back for the silly string and the fake playdo."

THE CRAZY WORLD OF MEDICINE   by Jay Vincent

FINBACKS ON THE UNIT
"Yes, we're lawyers for the injured and no we're not here to have our, uh,
fins removed."

THE CRAZY WORLD OF MEDICINE | by Jay Vincent

PAPERWORK FIRST!

"I don't care how long you've been waiting or that you're wearing a Stop Sign, you're not seeing the doctor until you do this paperwork!"

THE CRAZY WORLD OF MEDICINE   by Jay Vincent

WRONG DIRECTION

"Jeez, Frank, I said forward, go forward, that means away from the building and all you want to do is play with the siren."

THE CRAZY WORLD OF MEDICINE   by Jay Vincent

NEUROSURGEONS AT LARGE

"Well, men, they may not have confidence in us as surgeons but they'll
be damned impressed by our amazing alligator shoes and these three
feet long neckties. That's the important thing, right?"

THE CRAZY WORLD OF MEDICINE   by Jay Vincent

FUN WITH SAMPLES

The mystery of the missing urine samples went unsolved until Nurse Bob smiled, revealing two rows of perfectly yellow teeth.

THE CRAZY WORLD OF MEDICINE   by Jay Vincent

"Men, call CNN, I think we've found Jimmy Hoffa."

THE CRAZY WORLD OF MEDICINE by Jay Vincent

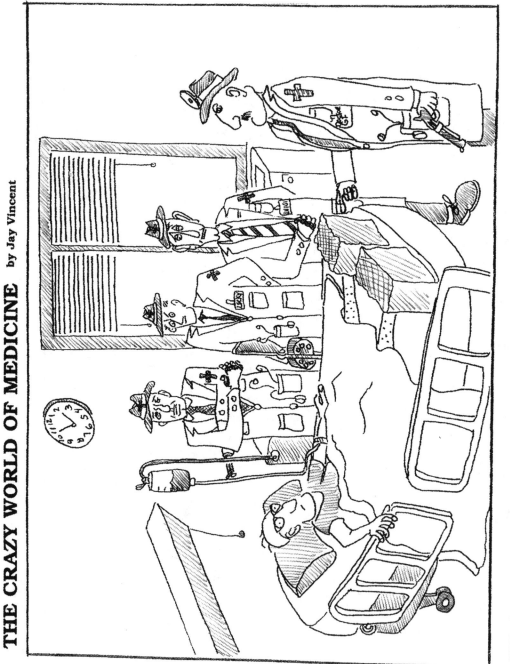

THE GODFATHER AND HIS CRONIES TAKE UP MEDICINE
"All right, these concrete shoes, it's all part of a treatment you can't refuse -
literally."

THE CRAZY WORLD OF MEDICINE by Jay Vincent

THE HATE FILLED PRESENTATION

"Now, these unique frames are more suitable for the likes of our hospital Presidents, especially considering the cheap, damn cheap, wages they grudgingly gave us," Housekeeper Carla said, her teeth clenched in a massive death bite.

THE CRAZY WORLD OF MEDICINE by Jay Vincent

TAKE A FLIGHT

"Whoa, looks like Crazy Al, the Gift Shop clerk, is at it again overfilling balloons with too much helium. Next he'll break out the B B gun. Will he ever quit?"

THE CRAZY WORLD OF MEDICINE by Jay Vincent

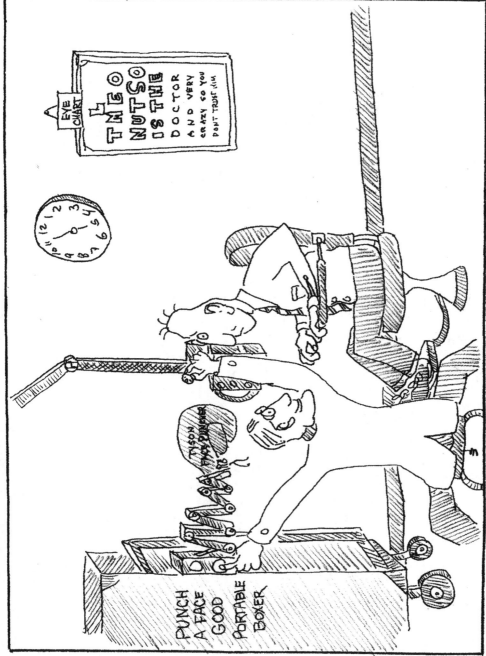

THE EYE TEST
"Oh, Mr. Cappy, you don't have to worry about that unsettling blast of air on your eyeball, this device goes way beyond that. You'll see!"

THE CRAZY WORLD OF MEDICINE   by Jay Vincent

TROUBLE WITH CATHETERS
Another rowdy Texas catheter up and kickin'

THE CRAZY WORLD OF MEDICINE | by Jay Vincent

WHOA! CENSUS IS DOWN

With patient census down drastically, staff resorted to other populations to meet the shortage and soon they were flocking in from everywhere, if not for treatment, then for the corned beef and cabbage in the cafeteria.

THE CRAZY WORLD OF MEDICINE

by Jay Vincent

DOCTOR, CONTROL YOURSELF!

Delighted that she'd gotten all the letters right, Doctor Goodeye suddenly lept forward and threw Mrs. Splurgeandbuy into a flying full Nelson. Thank God this was a full body contact office !

THE CRAZY WORLD OF MEDICINE by Jay Vincent

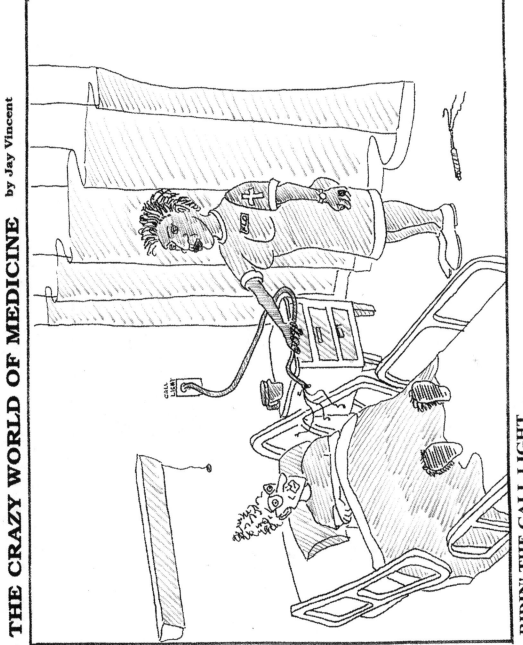

RIDIN' THE CALL LIGHT
"Now, Mrs. Hackleback, here's your call light for the one hundredth time and do feel free to use it as much as possible."

THE CRAZY WORLD OF MEDICINE by Jay Vincent

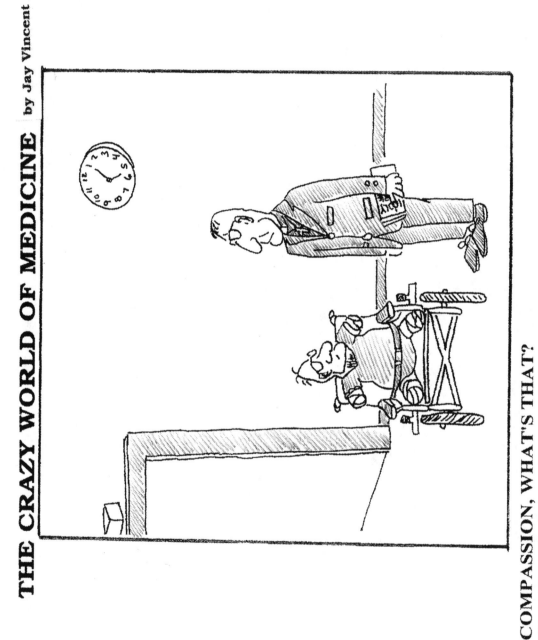

COMPASSION, WHAT'S THAT?

"Lost four limbs, eh? Well, at least the bright side is that you probably weigh a lot less. Now, were you tryin' to lose weight or what?"

THE CRAZY WORLD OF MEDICINE by Jay Vincent

HOT HEADED FLO NIGHTINGALE

"So, the nursing historians cleaned it up because, and get this, it was really, *lady throws a lamp* and yes, it happened more often than you might think."

THE CRAZY WORLD OF MEDICINE
by Jay Vincent

IS THAT THE PATCH YOUR WEARING?
"Don't worry Nurse Green, I may have smashed my cigarette against my forehead but I think I've got a brilliant idea," Doctor Blort blurted out banefully.

THE CRAZY WORLD OF MEDICINE   by Jay Vincent

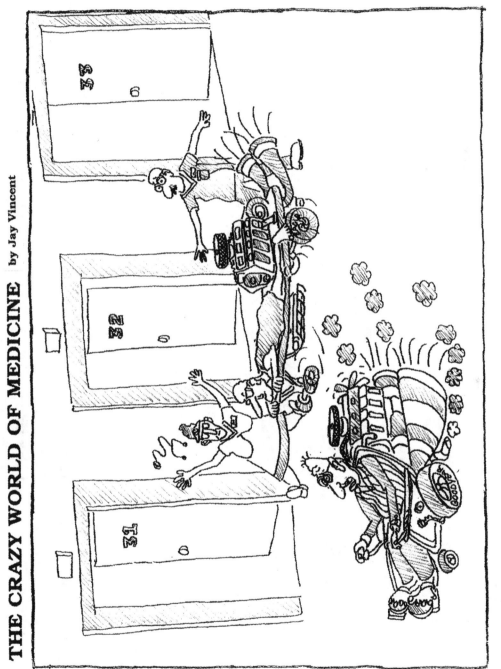

NASCAR GURNIES
Suddenly, the supercharged wheelchairs cut the corner, burning rubber on the Nursing home carpet, causing Nurse Maude to nearly wet her pants.

THE CRAZY WORLD OF MEDICINE | by Jay Vincent

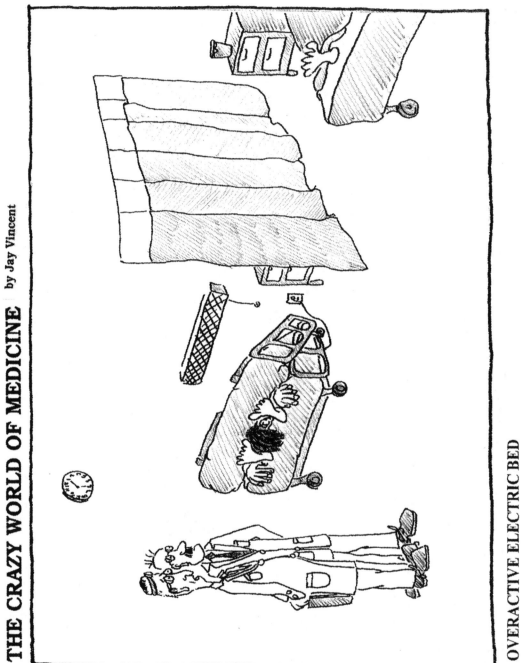

OVERACTIVE ELECTRIC BED

"Gosh, Hank, looks like your gallbladder patient has met with the mystical patient sandwich fate. Damn those irritable beds!

THE CRAZY WORLD OF MEDICINE by Jay Vincent

MAKING YOUR TOES FEEL BETTER

Doctor Heel, the Podiatrist, dispensed with tradition and began sporting the foot covered lab coat only to realize that it gave new meaning to the idea of being "walked all over".

THE CRAZY WORLD OF MEDICINE by Jay Vincent

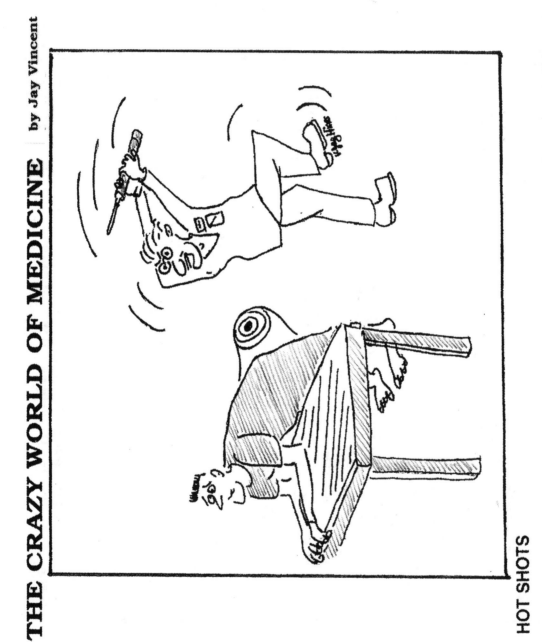

HOT SHOTS

Tired of being scoffed at for his fear of butts and needles, Male Nurse Dollert proved he was no slacker and gave his next injection with plenty of gusto.

THE CRAZY WORLD OF MEDICINE by Jay Vincent

FUN WITH GAS

Acting on a bet, Dentist Bob suddenly lept forward and gassed Nurse Plunkett.

THE CRAZY WORLD OF MEDICINE — by Jay Vincent

THE HAIR DOCTOR
Poor Tommy was traumatized when Doctor Goodspeed's combover suddenly
lost control and flew from his head.

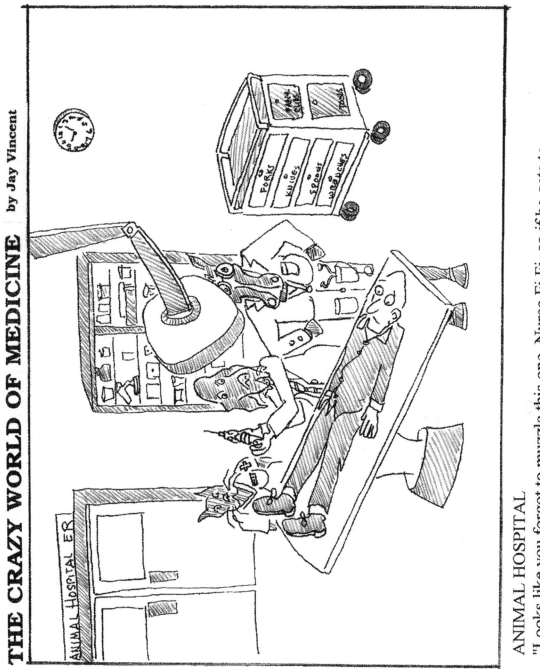

THE CRAZY WORLD OF MEDICINE   by Jay Vincent

ANIMAL HOSPITAL
"Looks like you forgot to muzzle this one, Nurse Fi Fi, so if he gets to bitin', it's your hide."

THE CRAZY WORLD OF MEDICINE by Jay Vincent

PRANK STAT CALL
"Hah, hah, he sure got here in a hurry. That stat call thing really does work!"

THE CRAZY WORLD OF MEDICINE   By Jay Vincent

ADMINISTRATOR GONE NUTS

Overstressed from an OP's call gone bad, Mr. Bard suddenly burst from his office dressed as his mother-in-law and dared anyone to laugh at his bird-print dress and frilly hat.

THE CRAZY WORLD OF MEDICINE by Jay Vincent

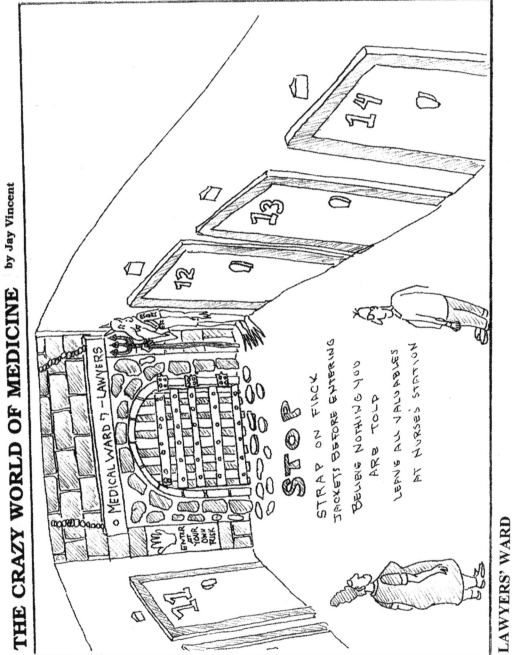

LAWYERS' WARD

"Got to keep 'em separate from the other patients or they'll have 'em suing each other. These guys are drumming up representation right on the medical unit."

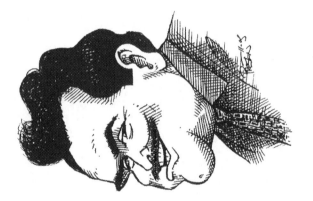

THE AUTHOR AND ILLUSTRATOR
JAY VINCENT

Jay Vincent is also the author of the Robert Boston Spy Series and the soon to be published series called The Adventures of the Park Street Hounds. The Crazy World of Medicine is based on real life experiences witnessed by the author who is also a medical professional. Also watch for the release in 2006 of The Crazy World of Medicine: The Madness Continues; The Crazy World of Medicine: The Madness Never Ends; and The Crazy World of Lawyers: The Court Goes Wild. Jay Vincent lives, writes, and illustrates in Michigan.

HERE'S AN OFFER FOR YOU

SELECT YOUR FAVORITE CRAZY WORLD OF MEDICINE ILLUSTRATION

HAVE IT FRAMED

HAVE IT IN COLOR

HAVE IT SIGNED BY THE ILLUSTRATOR

AND IT ONLY COSTS $14.95

Name of Illustration _____ pg no. _____

Send check of money order to:

The Crazy World of Medicine
P.O. Box 4141
Flint, Michigan 48504

Copies of this book can be ordered directly from Crazy World Productions